SKYFALL

YOUR HEART WILL FALL TOO

DEEPAK GUPTA

For my Mom, Poonam Rani –

No one has ever given more loving and unconditional support than I have been given by you. There is nothing sacred than God and Mom in this World.

I love you, too

About The Book

Don't see the world from the road,
  You would end your life,
  Living in the huge crowd,
  See the world from the sky,
  Then you will understand,
  How high you can fly.

How far can a Dad go to save his family? How far you and I can go? It may be a hypothetical question but what you would do when things become much complicated than never happened before. We want to save everyone but sometimes God doesn't want to. David and his family lived in Snag, Canada, where snowfall prediction was the much-complicated than any other decision. They were the happy family with hate and love but one day God showed the dynamism they never expected. How God could much cruel to destroy and create the same world again. Why God is still not satisfied with us and wants a new beginning. Something strange happened in Canada that never happened before and it was nothing but the heart falling Skyfall.

Prologue

Her face looked same as I remembered a few years ago. My eyes had captured her badly but why I am not seeing her happy smiling face even after spending a long time with her. I really don't remember the time when I laughed for the last time but sometimes, I smile to make others happy and to love their smiling eyes.

"Sometimes the most precious things become the ordinary things and the most precious things become the ordinary things."

We think God writes our destiny but it's not always universally true. I never wanted to lose the things as I lose so early. *I never imagined the day that would change everything in my happy life.* I wanted to grow, to fly high like an eagle but never wanted to grow like a person who doesn't even know about humanity. To become human, we must learn humanity and to understand God we must learn the dynamism of nature. We have to carry out the emotions which always keep us alive, keep our relationships alive but sometimes we face the situations which we never imagined even for our enemies as well. At the same time, we are happy and at another we become sad, it's because of the situations we face. I am David, an unlucky person and I think the most common citizen of the snag, Canada. Purchasing a coffee is like purchasing an Audi for me. My family has really different aspirations for me but they never understand me. I only wanted to keep them happy and to see their happy faces but I think they were searching happiness somewhere else.

"Some words should be unsaid so that we can still make our healthy relationship alive even after so many complaints in

our heart."

God made the beautiful life of heaven and hell, those who fly high reached the heaven and those who don't bury under the hell. *Be alive but don't with the poor inspirations. Sometimes it's better to die with some beautiful lessons than to get alive with an unknown face.*

CHAPTER ONE

Winter-Spring 2018
Heavy Snowfall
Snag, Canada
9:30 Sunday Morning

"Ugh! You are still the unluckiest and an unemployed person! Olivia, my wife growled, darted newspapers on my massive unshaven face. My dark black hairs drizzle in the air little bit settled too soon."

I was on the wooden sofa cracked from everywhere, lost its lustre and gazing like a dull trash. There was nothing new about it.

I yawned and allowed her to continue the same lecture I listened every day.

"I never thought that I would be married to a guy who doesn't even care for his responsibilities, she accused annoyingly. But still you don't know anything; even you don't even bother about our little children."

"I was still smiling, hiding my face just behind the white lustrous pages of my interesting novel. There was nothing innovative in this lecture, I mumbled in my dumb mind to save myself again."

"David, are you listening to me? Olivia howled at me loudly."

I was reacting like, I am reading the novel but actually, I was not. My eyes were gazing at the words, stealing my haunted house. These creepy things were accumulated by my grandfather. When he died, we took over the things but we didn't get anything more than a gift of emotions and priceless antiques. Yes yes! It was antiques. My grandfather was a studious man and he loved to roam around the world and that's why they left nothing for us. They lived lavishly but we were living in extreme penniless condition. I was not so genius like him, even I couldn't compare because I never listened and take care of the precious words which he always spoke to me.

We always crave for things, especially my wife Olivia. She worked throughout the day to earn few pennies and I was the maid to take care of our children. Oh no! You can even laugh on this matter, but I know I was a careless maid. I washed utensils and clothes every day and made breakfast for everyone. I take care of the bath of our newborn winsome baby Devin and of everything which a good mom does; even I was doing all the work of a woman but only things are, I was pretending to be a man who does anything except doing a good job and sometimes I never ashamed. I mumbled these words but never came out with the fog of my words and still freeze inside me.

"Dad! Dad! My daughter pearl, slightly red coloured, blushed smile everywhere with new hope and beginnings, which was just twelve years old sounded while picked my sapphire jeans, slashed from everywhere."

"My old doll has broken. Her hairs are not much glossy as before. I want a new beautiful doll for my upcoming birthday. I want to eat delicious chocolate cake on my birthday; Pearl demanded, turned and holds my neck conditionally from behind."

"Cake was always the luxurious foam of bread for us, I mumbled sadly."

"I would take it my dear daughter; I lied and blinked my eyes to give her a positive gesture, just to keep her happy."

I reminded when I promised her to give beautiful diary on her last birthday and even, I come up with but it was not an expensive diary and how she accepted her with happiness. *I could tell the lie but her eyes were saying the real truth and I never forgot that moment, the moment that taught me that happiness is priceless.* Good intentions never disappoint us, if we are brave enough to move forward.

Is there any law not to tell lies just to keep our family happy? I know that were hollow lies but those hollow lies were much better than to live without any hope.

My hollow lies were making our life like the flying mirage clouds; I was waiting for the rain but in the desert of the snow.

I could earn much for my family. I tried every second, every minute, every hour, every day and every moment for my family but I was stuck with my family and my destiny. Their love was much more to keep me trying even without any expectation. I was suffering from an endless hope. I talked one of my friends to give me any work in a garage even I asked many of my friends but they never gave me and ignoring me like a useless person. Are we much bound to the status? Olivia trusts me but her trust was shattering every day like my hope and that's why I hesitate much to tell my words, sometimes lies or truth in front of her to prove myself.

"David, I can't trust you more. You have been saying since this from the time we got married. We have three children now and one of them is still a newborn. We need clothes, plenty of milk, toys and books for him. Where do you get all these things and what about our future? She frowned few things even in less than one breathe, which was taking my breathe heavily."

She was not changed in fact exclusively same as I met her in college but I think I was changed. The fire inside our hearts was burning continuously like every day but the wooden fire inside the furnace was going to extinguish in few minutes.

Oh, shit, I muttered.

This furnace was our lifeline burns even more than 24 hours a day. It was looking like a kiln but we don't bother even if it looks like trash, we even don't bother. We have to save ourselves from the life taking dangerous temperature and that's really enough!

Woods were already turned into dark black coal. I threw my novel on the table which slid a little bit forward unintentionally and stood up from the broken sofa to bring some dry wood to fuel the fire of furnace from our veranda surrounded by heavy snow. Olivia's eyes were still starring me, tonelessly, waiting for her relevant questions but I ignored because I don't want my family to shiver in this all-time winter.

"Dad! My second son Ronan, neither senior nor younger among my children said eagerly, blinking his brown eyes. I am also coming, Dad! He declared astonishingly in his soft voice, didn't give me any chance to say no and dominated at me successfully."

He picked my left hand curiously with his tiny right hand good enough to wrap my two fingers tightly to confirm good safety. He was expecting terrifying adventure with me, but outside, the adventure was more than that. I opened the crushed wooden door of our house and an extreme flow of cool wind stunned both of us for a while.

We had to wake up early every day to clean the snow around our wooden house; otherwise, we would get locked inside our house and die. Death was always around us, little bit carelessness was much costly than anything else in this world. Is there something more worthy than our life?

"Dad, there's too much cold outside, he said, a little bit scared, put his left hand near the mouth to warm his hand. That was really low temperature. We don't have any temperature measurement machine on our table to get the right temperature because of Ronan always scared of that, but I was good enough to feel the accurate temperature along with washing utensils and clothes the whole day.

His legs were trembling to move any step forward. I picked him tightly to give him some bravery but I know he was very naughty just like my grandfather."

What about him? I was not even in the position to hold my head still in this chilling winter. Our eyes were not getting still, struggling every second. Finally, I gathered some latent bravery to move ahead.

"You are my son Ronan, let's bring out the wood, otherwise we would get freeze and I think we don't want it, I insisted with the bravery to motivate my son to move forward his step."

He wore the white cap made of animal fur which was covering him up to the ears and I had worn the gloves and a woollen brown cap to keep me safe from this mind freezing wind. The snow was falling like the cotton falling on the eve of Christmas.

Our legs were still trembling, unable to still and hold normally. We were outside He holds my hand tightly to confirm his safety again. It was just like we locked into the same small cage. Every step was looking like a mile for us. The snow was around three and a half feet deep from the surface which was covering our legs up to the thigh. The temperature was not looking like the same as every day we saw. Something was strange but extreme fall in temperature was in the snag. We ignored, took it normally and move forward.

"Dad! Dad! Mom is looking angry today. Why don't you make her favourite dish? She really loves fish and I love too and he smiled innocently which I always love him. Dad please can we eat fish today? He picked my right leg stubbornly for a while."

My ten-year-old son Ronan was totally behaving like a young person. Every time he looked at me, he changed my mood in just one blink, and I think that's the attribute God has given to the most loving children. He was much intelligent than me, I mumbled to myself, accumulating some of the beautiful moments. His smile was my daily medicine to wake up to new hope every day. I love the way he crawled into my room and said, "Dad! I am frightened. Oh! I really love the way. There's a ghost in my room and he always wanted to stick to my chest and how I cover him always with the wings of my shoulder to give him warm love and I think that's the reason they were much closer to me than their hard-working mom."

We reached the back side of our wooden house, wandering in the veranda, picking the most suitable and dry wood for our furnace. Our veranda was never looked like the beautiful garden full of flowers and sweet fragrance because snowfall never allowed us to do so. Ronan was picking up the tiny dry sticks for the chimney. How small things make the big changes in life. I was still unhappy with me but not with my life. I took the one deep breathe and put the log of wood on my right shoulder, and this was much lighter than the weight of the responsibility of my life, from which I had been struggling for a long time.

Dad! Look at the sky; he screamed, a little bit confused and his sound became an echo in microseconds. The log slipped and fell from my heavy shoulder.

Oh my god, Jesus! I sounded the words unintentionally to bring out my astonishment and little bit terror. Extreme huge black clouds were moving like they were above our head. I had never seen such giant clouds in my whole life. It was not looking like the unexceptional clouds as it was giant, dark and much peculiar from the clouds we saw every day. I could see the lighting stamped just like the scars in the sky. It was an extremely haunting sight. Ronan picked my hand hard, gasped his breathe, as he always loved me like a superhero who can do anything like an iron man. He thought I can fly as high I can, fight with unending enemies and can help any other unconditionally.

"Look at the sky dad, clouds are moving so swiftly. Where's the sun dad? When it would rise, He panted while expecting the good answer from my cold frozen lips and even his eyes were still waiting for my answer, but I had an unanswered question."

I didn't know what was happening. So many questions were surrounded me like the unending questions of Olivia every day. The climate was changing quickly even more than any normal day. Our fingers were getting frozen, demanded the wildfire. I picked the Ronan and the wooden log swiftly and ran towards the wooden gate of our home.

I shut the door aloud and threw the wood log on the floor. We both were gasping for our breathing. We looked each other with a smile, reminding the good adventure we saw a few seconds ago. That was like the Dad son connection and only we could understand it. Olivia was in the chair, fitted smoothly with the table, moving her legs randomly and cutting shiny black fish for our lunch. I

I was decorating the woods inside the extinguished furnace. We could stop anything but not the fire of this chimney. I sprinkled the spirit on the perfectly arranged woods and threw a lighted matchstick on it. I stood up, a little bit confused and still watching the heavy giant clouds from the translucent window, feeling the negative vibes and this time I picked the newspaper to read the daily news excited me much well than novels.

CHAPTER TWO

Aero Department
Snag, Canada
10:30 Sunday Morning
Same day

"Three helicopters have crashed, we would also die, need help! *Mayday! Mayday!* Please copy that, please copy that, one of the helicopter pilots, struggling with the wind, yelled in the mike with his trembling hand. Mayday! Mayday! We need help. Our helicopter is going to crash in few minutes. We need help, said continuously with some hope in his eyes"

They were flying high at an altitude of around 5000 feet. Their helicopter was swinging in deliberately into the random directions with the swift atmospheric pressure. Their faces were much frightened like the people before hugging the terrific death.

"Do you copy? He yelled again and tried to make a successful contact with the "Aero department." We are stuck inside the loop of the heavy blizzard and getting lost in the black clouds swiftly. Mayday! We need help. He looked at the fuel indicator giving him the bad news he never heard."

"Fuel is going to end in few minutes. We need another helicopter for help, he demanded with some hope. We have already lost our direction. Nothing is clear in front of us.

We are flying above snag 80 degrees north."

Their strong green helmets, reflecting safety, were waving up into the random directions due to the heavy atmospheric pressure the situation was out of control, which was creating hypertension. They were trained to not to get panic but how could you expect no panic when someone is facing his own death. How Ridiculous! Thunderstorms and blue sharp lighting were clearly seen from their helicopters.

Our faces are freezing, please help us! Did you copy? Mayday please mayday! He said repeatedly to establish a better communication with the commander of the aero department.

"James listens; we would die in few minutes. Now we can't do anything. Do you have any last wish? I think this is the end of our beautiful journey, Arnold, our copter captain announced in the strict voice."

"Yes captain, but I want a new life again, he mumbled in low sad voice."

"I didn't hear James, Arnold asked again."

"Yes captain, James replied in strict voice ignored his last wish."

Their chopper had caught fire in the air, even in the frozen wind. The engine has stopped now struggling to ignite continuously. They were screaming hard in between the black clouds, but there was no one to listen to them. Suddenly they listened the voice disturbing continuously which was coming from the receiver, getting dead in just a few seconds.

"Copter 250, we are listening, we copy that, we copy that, one of the office coordinators replied in hurry, a little bit stunned."

"We have crashed! Arnold screamed. It's too late. It was really an irrational response."

The helicopter caught fire into the air, struggling to blast soon. The back side of the copter was already damaged and crushed awfully. Instantaneously it blasts with the high pressure just like the nuclear bomb blast in the heavy windy air. If they did not die even of big explosion then they would surely die with the robust echo of the horrible blast.

"Copter 250, Hey! Hey! We copy that, we copy that, the coordinator asked again with some unending hope, inside terrified."

And this time no voice came out from the receiver. The big explosion had already given his answer

"Sir! No answer, we have tried so many times, the coordinator declared to the navy officer."

"There's no evidence of the four helicopters which were flying over the snag, Coordinator sounded, and setting his black lustrous mike around his diamond looked face. Sir! The temperature is declining swiftly. There is the very big change in the climate of snag till now. Should we contact weather department to know about this gradual decrease?"

"We should wait, Mr Pack. Our many flights are still on their way. This may create rumours among the people. Tell me about the reports of other planes and the report of crashed ones as well, the captain asked while burning his brown cigar with the lighter in just one jerk."

"Don't do anything before I instructed, he threatened."

Yes sir! The coordinator shook his head silently.

******

"David, our delicious crispy fish curry is ready now. I think we have the beautiful day today except for my boring lecture! So sorry dear! I am really very very sorry! She apologized and smiled to regain the beautiful moments again."

Usually, I cooked food in the house but Olivia sometimes cooked food on weekends. She cooked rarely on demand and made delicious food and that's why she made food on the weekends when our children got bored with the same taste of food cooked by me. Ugh! I was not the bad cook as you think.

"Sweetheart! Look, there's not even a ray of sunlight today. The weather was really stunning as we expected on weekends Snow was falling like the giant heavy stones falling from the sky, beating our house, I said eagerly. Listen, Olivia! Like someone is beating our wooden house. Listen! Listen! Suddenly a drastic voice teased our ears like someone filled us with despair. It was just like a massive earthquake."

We got panicked, a little bit curious to know the matter.

"Oh shit! Olivia, what was that? I screamed doubtfully."

"Was it an earthquake? I stood up suddenly to check the matter!"

"Olivia take care of our Pearl and Ronan and doesn't come out till I don't ask. Do I need to check what was that? I ordered to her."

I ran swiftly towards the veranda to find out the mysterious thing, which shook our house and hearts heavily. I was searching for those creepy things, blowing my hands to keep it warm. My legs were partially inside the soft snow, not allowing me to move forward, frozen up to the joints and crawling to find out the cause of the sudden deep jerk which damaged our wooden house.

Suddenly I got stunned; my legs didn't allow moving forward.

"Olivia, I yelled in the thick voice. My mouth fell open waiting for her. There was some peculiar thing burning and fluxing negligently in the back side of our veranda."

She came out swiftly, a little bit scared and astonished to check the matter. Ronan and Pearl were also running with her.

I grabbed the hoe rapidly and throwing soft snow upon the burning yellow flames. Olivia, Ronan and pearl were doing the same, but with their bare hands. I was a little bit worried, thinking about how this thing fell into the veranda but really more than for my family. How do they become shield when things become worse! In few minutes we controlled the fire and extinguished it completely. Our faces were getting red swollen due to the extreme snowy wind. I picked the partial fire burnt part from the surface and it was written "Copter 250". I thrilled to find the part of the helicopter in my house. Inside tensed, I picked our both children swiftly and ran towards the wooden gate to enter the house.

"Olivia it was the part of "Copter 250", I gasped and struggle for breathing. We should call the snag police right now."

Pearl and Ronan were crying hard as their hands were red swollen and burning due to the sensation of hot and cold temperature. Enormous cold ice froze their bare hands completely. My eyes got heavy with tears and Olivia had seen tears in my red eyes, still, I controlled my tears so well like a good dad and cuddled both of them tightly. I think there was no good cure better than this and kissed the frozen palm of their hands."

Magic Magic!

I chanted while making the weird faces.

Magic! Magic!

thermometer.

"David, we can't leave our house, she declared without completing me my statement. You know everything. We don't have anything to stay anywhere in the whole Canada. We can't leave our house and that will be good for us."

"And really significant than the life of our family, I blanched, frustrated inside. Look at this temperature. The temperature was four degree just five minutes ago; now see its two degree Celsius. It's not strange Olivia, it's very much strange. We should leave the snag right now."

"But where would we go? We don't have money. We don't have much food. Are you really going to do this? Olivia spluttered. Have you lost your mind? You can leave the home, but we would not. You never cared for us! And a couple of tears fell down from Olivia's eyes, rolled down her soft cheeks. She was not much emotional stable and that's how sometimes she dominated me very well."

"Ronan! Pack your significant belongings and ask your mom that we are leaving, I ordered. Pearl we are not going to take any of your toys and I am really very sorry for this. I was in hurry to leave the house because the negative vibes were making the tornado of horrible stories in my mind."

"We are not going anywhere! Olivia shouted, stunned me for few seconds. You listen; we are not going anywhere, she repeated. Do you really care for us? Then leave us alone, Please! Please! Much stressed."

I was much embarrassed, why they didn't listen to me, much frustrating inside.

I planned to leave the home tonelessly, inside lost in despair and much wrenched, not with them but with my behaviour. I was feeling very guilty as I had never taken care of my family. I never take care of their needs and I think this was the real culprit of my life. I made the gesture to go without any indication to come again. I opened the shattered door with my unwanted hands and took my jacket. Pearl was still looking at me. I bring the tears in her eyes as well. I think she understood me much better than my wife. I left home without uttered any single word but still had many words locked inside my frozen heart.

CHAPTER THREE

Snag, Canada

11 o clock Sunday Morning

I was crawling silently with my unwanted legs, hands locked inside the pocket, on the slippery road covered with the snow. There were no leaves on the trees, already shattered due to heavy snow. I was looking at the shattered trees without any unwanted attention. The road was much empty than my hollow heart. Huh! How could I be much crazy to leave my children alone at home? I yelled ay own self, much flooded with the spiral of thoughts. I am the poorest dad of this world. My eyes were still wet with the tears, waiting to be warm with the love of my family. My heart wanted to stop me, but my mind wanted to move on.

No one stopped me, I cursed me insanely. Am I much worse than anyone else? I am the worst dad of this world, repeated the same line to dip myself in despair. I was so much angry at me. My legs were trembling and heart sinking for a while. I saw the red seat like God has made for me. I took the seat in the corner of the tree whose leaves were already shed, totally barren like me.

In between I was blaming myself; I heard the thrilling sound, teased my ears completely. A huge crowd was running towards me, utterly scared. I couldn't see their faces but in unison, they were looking extremely horrible. I got scared, managed and controlled myself. Why were they coming towards me? The snow was shaking under my feet on the ground and resulting in the sharp crack in the frozen ice. They all were walking swiftly towards me, ignoring my attention. I stood from the frozen bench abruptly to know the matter, zoomed my eyes a little bit to see the crowd clearly and the scene I saw stunned me completely from head to toe. People were also coming out from the premises to join the crowd abruptly. Some were running carelessly; some fell on the slippery road, managing themselves. Children crying were seemed too creepy and horrible at that time. Finally, I locked my fist for a while to hold my courage.

My unconscious mind got conscious when I saw the blizzard of ice coming towards me with the random huge crowd. The voice of crowd was much powerful than any loudspeaker, cleverly teasing my ears completely. I tried to run and suddenly slipped on the slippery ice with my head stuck with the hard ice and got helpless. My head got the deep cut on the right corner, completely jumbled me for few seconds. Blood was felling, rubbed on my face completely and my hands were also rubbed on the sharp hard ice. The skin has vanished from my right hand. The crowd was waiving hands at me, but I was partially dead unable to help myself. I tried to stand up but slipped again unintentionally. Lost in the anonymous universe, in just one jerk, the face of pearl flashed in my unconscious mind. It was like someone has put an anecdote of energy into my whole body. I smiled in deep pain to regain my energy. I tried to stand up again, but the big striking bergs of ice beat me from back heavily, the crowd passed me so abruptly and swiftly with no indication of any halt. My back got hit by the giant bully icebergs. It was just like the moment that someone has stitched hundreds of bullets into my back one after one. My back was swollen, frozen and draining in dark blood freeze upon it like the random paining. The crowd fell on the slippery ground, hit by the icebergs. People were struggling to save their loved ones, terrified, stressed and felt like baffled by nature. Many were lying on the road in hope, waiting for help; even some of them were partially dead, lost their lives including me. My eyes were getting heavy after each and every second and there was a big clever smile on my dark blood-coated teeth waiting for the death. My body was getting freeze. My legs and hands declined to move even a single step. I was sleeping in my own dreams peacefully, somewhere lost in my own heaven after this unforeseen hell. Death was whispering and chanted some magic in my mind to leave the body but I think, I was not ready for that.

Waked from my own dream, suddenly someone put his heavy shoe leg on my injured back and I bounced a little bit in the snowy air. It was really the heavy jerk to keep me awake from the dead but that jerk showed me some reaming connection with the earth and prevented me to sleep in the deadly two-degree temperature.

"I can't die like this, I furiously yelled at myself to regain my lost life. My family is waiting for me. I can't die like this."

I stood up with my latent courage to get the way to reach my home. I have covered five miles just before I left my home, lost in my own thoughts. My body was almost dead, but my soul was not allowing me to death. I looked around me; there was the moment of whopped everywhere. People were crying endlessly, terrifying and panicked. There were Dead bodies everywhere, seemed to like a big graveyard with open bodies everywhere. I was much worried about my family. How were they? Are they all right? A lot of thoughts were wandering around my blurry eyes. I ignored every negative thought, accumulated some courage and managed my way to walk along the one side of the road. My legs were not good enough to walk swiftly, but my inner soul wanted to. I was walking in my uneven random gesture, controlling my legs well enough. People were still looking at me strangely hoping for some help. I was ignoring each and every injured man and woman like a selfish person but my eyes got thrilled when I saw a girl fell carelessly on the road, partially injured with eyes closed without any indication of his guardians. Blood was flowing from her head, making way for her small pony, locked tightly with a red ribbon. Her white dress had become red entirely covered with the thick sticky blood.

Hey hey! You okay! I demanded some sign of life. Hey! Listen, you girl. She was not much conscious but her deep breathing gave me a sign of relief. A lot of blood was still flowing from her pony. I tore one part of my white shirt and folded it around her head abruptly. Her body was much cold than I thought. She was totally frozen and needed heat but why I was caring for her. My whole family was much far away from me. There were a lot of people who were dying on the bed of the hard ice. How many I can care. A deep thought was still wandering in my tensed mind. I wanted to leave her but I didn't know why I was caring for her. I brought her into my both hands unthinkingly. I picked her hand and it was frozen. I opened the first two buttons of my shirt and put her hands on my warm injured chest. I think that was much warmer for her. Her cold hands reminded me my daughter Pearl. I was running even more than my capacity on the slippery road. A lot of thoughts were still wandering in my mind, not leaving me even for one second. The love and hate of my wife Olivia, the blushed face of my daughter, Ronan smartness and my little one-year-old carelessly on the road.

Dad, suddenly a voice echoed from the one side of the road. I thought it was just a hallucination, but when I saw my daughter Pearl on the other side of the road, my eyes got blushed and wet at the same time, the tears of happiness hugged my cheeks. I ran swiftly towards her to finish this unending journey. I cuddled her tightly, washing my eyes completely. The fur of her jacket kissed me beautifully to welcome my presence.

Dad! Blood is flowing, she whispered, blowing her warm breath on the deep cut of my head and she chanted, Magic! Magic! And her sweet voice gave an unending peace to my mind.

"Where is Olivia? I asked."

Someone picked my leg from behind. He was my son Ronan and Olivia were starring me behind him.

"Your head is bleeding David! She demanded an answer, inside little bit apologising and bring out the medicine box from the bag. My legs didn't allow me to stand and I fell to the ground."

Dad! Pearl screamed!

"Are you okay David?"

Ronan bent down on his little legs.

I was on the thigh of Olivia. She was crying, stunning inside and a couple of her warm tears fell on the deep cut wound of my head. It was much better than any other medicine. Her warm tears healed my head in just a few seconds. Sometimes in between love, things come and disappeared quickly and whole life is required to understand the real love.

"David! I am sorry, she apologised."

"Don't be, I replied, regaining the moment. She tore and wrapping the transparent cloth around my injured head.

Inside scared, I got up in the middle of the dressing. We need to leave Olivia! We need to leave! I repeated the same sentence again and again. I was reacting to an insane person. We need to leave. I picked her shoulder tightly.

"Olivia, where is Devin? I demanded a positive answer."

"Olivia where is Devin?"

"He died, she screamed."

"I slapped her hard, don't say these words for our baby and yelled at her again."

I fell on the ground to control my heavy tears. Her last few words had destroyed me completely.

"What had happened Olivia? I asked with my trembling lips."

He died; and she hugged me tightly, screamed again and got unconscious in my bare injured hands. I stood up and ran to put her in the back seat of the car, took the children and a little bag. My eyes were already flushed with the tears and pain was lost into it for my little baby Devin, even I was much unfortunate to see his last face. I was really regretting myself to leave my family alone. This was the biggest mistake I want to correct but it was too late. Some mistakes can't be corrected and leave behind the deep impact of regretting each and every moment during the whole life. I took my seat with the lost attitude and drive the car carelessly, into the random directions, lost into death on the straight sharp road full of human dead bodies and frozen ice.

CHAPTER FOUR

Weather Department
Snag, Canada
12:30 Sunday Morning

"Ma'am! Snag's temperature is declining swiftly, we need to broadcast this information to everyone in the snag, one of the meeting managers requested, inside tensed"

Six people were in the big dark room, a little bit gloomy, on their respective comfortable chairs with their cold bare folded hands on the lustrous black table.

"We need to inform, he requested again, showing weather report to the head Ms Arden. Arden was walking around the circular table in an unending loop, with parallel lines of heavy tension on her head.

"Ridiculously, she closed to the manager, made eye contact and announced, we can't inform anyone."

"But ma'am, he replied, completely frightened. Others members are also waiting for your decision."

"We can't. You listened! We can't, she threatened in loud voice."

"We are human. We can do anything to save our lives, you understand! Anything means anything. They can kill or can be killed just to save themselves, to save their loved ones. If we inform them about the gradual decline in temperature, the situation would get worse. They all will try to leave Canada and of course we need to save all, but this is not the right time to inform anyone, she declared without a bit hesitation, ignored everyone's suggestion."

"But ma'am, please see this report, he interrupted again and handed over the report in the hands of Arden. This is the weather report of last two days and we have observed a gradual decline in temperature from eight degrees to minus three degree Celsius. I think this is not normal like the ordinary days. The extreme cold snowy winds are coming swiftly from Greenland and I think we need to look seriously into it. Glaciers are falling in Greenland and there's a fear of tsunami in Canada. If we would do anything then this would vanish the sign of human element in Canada. There is heavy blizzard coming every hour to Canada and we should leave Canada right now and I think everyone, he protested and announced without caring the opinion of others."

It was an irrational response by the team manager but he knew much better than Arden. Our position doesn't matter. It never matters where and how we work, but it matters how we present ourselves when others need us.

There was the moment of chaos in the meeting room. Everyone's faces were looking scared, little bit blank, confused and waiting for some positive outcome.

Stop it! I said stop it! Arden growled. No information would pass to citizens of Canada. This decision is only for the safety of our citizens and this is final. No further discussions expected. Meeting adjourned and she declared and threw the weather report file on the table, binds her bare hands and leaned towards the transparent window with the winning attitude.

Suddenly A man with some belief opened the door swiftly, halted his steps just inside the room. He was the handsome man with the shiny black overcoat on his shoulder, a deep beard diamond face, hairs creased in style, terrified face and some documents locked in his hands.

Everyone stood from their respective chairs surprisingly, mumbled words carelessly, hoping a good answer.

Hey! Who are you? She turned and yelled with the red face. How dare you enter the meeting of weather department? Security, she demanded, security.

"Ma'am I am Henry and I just want to talk about the gradual decline in temperature, he requested. I will take just a few minutes."

"But we won't. Get out, she declared."

"Ma'am this is about the life of people, I need to explain, and otherwise everything would end."

She ignored his opinion and demanded the security officers.

Two Security man hold him tightly from the back and he was managing to come out from their tight grip. Suddenly he punched both from his hard elbow picked the remote abruptly and opened TV.

Everyone got silent except the noise of snowy wind and TV news.

"Ma'am see this, thousands of persons have already frozen and died at snag. Look at their faces, their bodies got swollen and become hard as stone. You think its normal weather conditions, not much. They all have already slept in the Gulf of extreme cold death. This is not blizzard, this is Skyfall."

"Shh! Hey! What did you say? Arden said, confirming his words again."

Everyone got stunned. Their eyes were starring him without any eye blinking.

"What you said? She repeated."

Skyfall and he threw the thick book into the air, which landed and slid smoothly on the table, spread little bit fire of dust in the air.

Skyfall? Everyone laughed in the same tone.

"This is not a joke, Henry's voice got thick and serious. This book was written in the year 1918 by one of the scientists who lived in Greenland 100 years ago. Everyone got silenced, stunned and curious inside. 100 years ago, this type of extreme fall in temperature was observed in Greenland, land of ice. Once there was life possible in Greenland and the normal temperature was about 5 to 10 degree Celsius. People were glad and living their life at that time just like us, but on 10th February 1918, the gradual decline in temperature was observed and there were few scientists who discovered to find out the problem of this fall, and after a long struggle they were succeeding in finding out the reason and it was Skyfall."

"So, how do you know about this life-saving book? One of the men interrupted him in the middle; straiten his eyebrows, curious to know the answer."

"Because my Dad was that one scientist, he sounded toneless, tensed inside. No one listened to him. Everyone thought, he was mad but they forgot that genius people are mad, sometimes much mad. He published the Skyfall book in the whole Greenland in just two days, tried to save the life of people in Greenland and even provided them for free and also published many articles as well, but weather department never listened to him, no one listens to him. Over three lakhs people died in this Skyfall in which two and a half lakhs bodies are still clueless. No one knows about the lost dead bodies. They are still frozen and buried under the deep hard ice. I think, People should leave Canada immediately, otherwise this would be the end of humankind and we would be responsible for this life taking reminded the words of his dad, "We are human. We can do anything to save our life, anything means anything." To reduce the weight of the life, someone kicked and pushed few people in the lift negligently and lift got closed. People were dying not because of the spiky cone-shaped ice but because of the fear of losing their lives. I never thought that I was the lucky one to save their life, but I was a little bit late, I think very late."

I crawled, but this time to reach the emergency stairs to leave the building as soon as possible. I stood up on my trembling legs again and gathered all my energy to walk down the stairs. People were rushing with me and it was not like walking but like falling on the stairs. Some persons fell on the stairs and other people were walking on their back without any sympathy. The scene was much horrible than I think. They were yelling in pain. Blood was sprinkled everywhere on the stairs and walls, but no one was caring. They thought, their life is much significant than the life of others and why did they? I was managing my control on the stairs and suddenly a lady in black formal uniform fell on me carelessly. Her right hand was injured and she was wishing to someone who could help her to get rid of this mess. Her poor face melted me easily and I picked her tightly on my left shoulder, maintaining my control with just one leg. Blood was still flowing from my head but I didn't have time to look on it. After twenty minutes of deep struggle, we were on the ground floor, walking towards the exit gate and the moment we saw thrilled and freeze our mind. No one was moving ahead of the exit gate. The spiky cone-shaped ice was still falling from the sky even much bigger than before. There were only ice swords everywhere on the road. If anyone moved forward, they would get killed in just one shot. It was much dangerous than any gun.

"Now, what can we do? She mumbled and looked at me strangely with her big eyes."

"Do you think I have an idea lady; Henry popped and looked at her."

People were rushing here and there and we were still talking cleverly. Oh shit! I was stuck with a girl, Ugh! He mumbled and controlled himself.

"You work here, he asked."

"She nodded tonelessly."

"Tell me Mr.........? Please! She yelled at him. She was bold enough to dominate on him."

"Mr Henry! And He completed her statement."

"Wait wait! He declared inside defensive and paused a little bit."

"Is there any washroom in this building? He questioned her, searching it here and there."

"We are stuck here and you want to go washroom, Mr Henry, she growled at him."

"Hey I am not your boyfriend or your husband, he yawned. Tell me fast where is washroom?

"Yes, even on this floor, she declared."

"Is there any bathtub in it?"

"Yes of course. Hey, what you want to do?" you want to bath right now. Are you okay? She said strangely in trembling voice."

"Come with me! He asked."

Hey, I will not come, she declared confidently.

"Come, please!

And he picked her hand tightly with my strong fingers."

We ran fast towards the washroom, ignored every disturbing element and he closed the door.

"Hey! Hey! Hey! Mr Open the door, she declined to stay and yelled at him very loudly."

"I need a big hammer, he said, ignored her demand again."

"What?"

"But I think it's in the tool room! She guessed."

"Can you take it?"

Yes! Why not! She answered with sarcasm. I am here to bring hammer in this tragedy.

"Bring it, please! We have very less time to escape."

"Okay, I am! Don't make weird faces, she said, accept her order.

"Should I come with you? He said.

I am good enough, don't worry, she smiled faking and leave."

After a couple of minutes, she left, someone knocked the door, I opened and a big bully man punched me on my nose, very hard. I fell on the ground, unconscious for a while. He was a bully man with a hammer; maybe he knew our plan already. He slammed the door swiftly and started hitting the corners of the bathtub with the generous power to bring it out and I was seeing everything, unable to move. In just a few seconds he brings out the bathtub which was sprayed with my dark red blood. I was still on the ground starring him and seeing everything but was deadly paralysed.

"Hey listen, don't dare to come in my way, he threatened me and picked the inverted bathtub on his head, good enough to hide his dumb face. He opened the door carelessly and suddenly the girl slammed the hammer on his genital part too hard. He felled on the ground with the bathtub without any sign to wake up again. The bathtub got cracked from the corners but still good enough for them to escape."

"You hit so hard! Don't you think he needed much less power hit than on his part? I said in sympathy."

"He actually deserves it, even more than this! She sounded and smiled cleverly. Leave him, what's the next step?"

"Wait to close the door, Henry said."

She slammed the door without asking any further question.

"We would take this bathtub inverted over our heads just like this bullshit guy, he said and kicked him hard."

Henry's nose was bleeding much but he ignored.

"We would not stop until we reach outside. We would not stop, whatever would be the situation, he said. People can do anything to save their life. Like, think thousands of killers are waiting for us outside. We need to escape from them. Are you ready? I expected a positive answer from her, inside much terrified."

"Okay don't teach me. Yes! She nodded."

The inverted bathtub was on our head. I was first in the row. We took the heavy deep breathe.

"Have you run in the marathon, he asked."

"Nopes, she replied."

"Now from today you will, he announced. Open the door"

She kicked the door and we rushed towards the exit gate at swift speed. We were yelling hard to prevent people in our way, but we were wrong. Some people at the exit gate rushed towards us unthinkingly. Our swift speed was much as we didn't control it and kicked directly in their faces unintentionally. Three people were kicked and injured by the tub, I think their jaws got broken and in barely twenty seconds we were on the slippery road flooded with conically shaped ice swords.

"Run! Run! Henry screamed."

People were not running towards us as the sky was still falling but many tried to and killed by heavy spiky shaped ice swords.

"Run we need to run fast, he said again."

Before we reached somewhere, a spiky cone-shaped heavy ice sword rubbed harshly on her right injured hand. Blood started to drip again from her hand.

"My right is broken. I can't walk anymore, she declared in pain. My hand is frozen now and bleeding much."

Before we took any decision, I saw a black car crawling towards us very slowly due to slippery ice on the road.

"We need your help! He requested to the driver. We need your help. We are deeply injured. Please open the door."

"I can't help you, try to understand, he said with no humanity."

"We are deeply injured, please open the door, otherwise we would die, open the door and he kicked on the door angrily."

"You can't do this, he yelled."

"Open it"

"I Can't"

We had lost our hope completely.

Suddenly the back door of the car opened by the lady who lay on the back seat.

"Come inside, she said calmly in low voice."

We threw the tub on the road, took heavy breathe, managed to enter the car and slammed the door swiftly.

"Olivia! David yelled at her with no sympathy. What you did?"

"David, if someone would think like me at that time when we were facing the blizzard, then our baby Devin would be with us today, he could be alive, she said, breathing heavily and few drops fell out from his red swollen eyes."

I was still silent like my mouth was stitched with pain.

downwards."

"Hey you listen, David panicked."

"Yeah! Oh, shit, the roof of the car is getting heavy due to the weight of the snow, Henry first confused and sounded. We need to remove the ice as soon as possible, otherwise, the roof would break down and we would die, again the roof got bulged downwards.

The strange unconscious girl got conscious before we took any action. Mom! Dad! She whispered slowly. Mom! Dad! These were the second few words told by her after I met her.

"We are going little girl, Olivia interrupted before the David say something."

"David, we need to come out from the car to remove ice from the roof as fast as possible, Henry declared in action."

"But how, we might get injured, David replied. We get killed in just one jerk of spikes of snow. What to do now?"

"Do you have the toolbox? Henry questioned."

"I don't know!"

"What do you mean I don't know? This is your car!"

"This is not my car, I stole it."

"You stole it?"

"How could you do this?"

"I could do this and yes for my family."

"You can do anything for your family?"

"Yes! Sometimes I can, David growled."

"Okay okay! Check if there is any toolbox at the back?"

"Okay!"

Suddenly the roof again got bulged downwards, much closer to us.

Have you found the toolbox? David screamed, demanded the toolbox right now.

"Yeah! Yeah! I found it."

Henry opened the box with his trembling fingers, controlling well and found the screwdriver. He opened all the screws of the right-side gate of the car.

"What you want to do? I questioned Henry, frightened inside!"

"We would use this gate as the shied to protect us from spikes of ice, Henry continued.

"Really! Okay, you have really a brilliant mind, I encouraged him."

"I am a scientist, Henry announced."

"Really handsome man? I replied sarcastically."

"Any doubt?"

"No, not after this! And they shared the clever smile even in this tough situation."

We came out from the car with the lavish big gate on our heads to protect us from razor blade ice swords.

"Will it work? I questioned him."

"Yes man! You didn't steal a car, he replied. You steal a luxury car. You know it has bullet-proof gates. Our heads can be broken but this gate can't be."

Marvellous! The strange girl interrupted, picked her hand tightly due to injury.

"You are still alive, Henry giggled."

"Yes, Mr Fortunately! She replied sounded cleverly."

We tried to remove the heavy berg of ice from the roof and united our entire energy to remove the giant berg.

"We are not able to replace the berg; Henry halted his hands a bit. This is very heavy and freezes on the roof. We need a sharp tool to remove this, otherwise, everything would end."

Olivia! I screamed, inside terrified and a heavy spiky cone ice injected into my hand and I fell on the ground in just one jerk, unable to control myself. Olivia got tensed.

Henry threw the gate on me abruptly to save myself from the spiky swords of ice and grabbed me by the car.

"Come inside, Henry ordered me, hoping to listen to him."

"David! Olivia got tensed serious face. I was unconscious and no voice was coming from me, signifying half death."

"David, please get up, Olivia ordered me again, but no response from me.

Suddenly Henry picked the door and fixed it tightly to save ourselves. He jumped so high to take the driving seat, tight the seat belt and set the gear to move forward.

"We have to remove the ice as fast as possible, Henry gasped, breathing heavily, asked the Olivia."

David was on the legs of Olivia. Blood was flowing negligently from his right hand. He was crying in pain and Olivia was trying to bring out the spiky of ice from his hand which was passed barely from his hand.

"It's not coming out; Olivia blanched, applying her whole force to bring the spiky of hard ice out. It's not coming out.

"Olivia! Don't do this and I gave my negative gesture to not to bring out the spiky to prevent the die-hard pain.

"We need to leave from here, the spiky cone-shaped ices have changed their direction, Henry announced, inside much scared."

"What! Olivia got astonished and again the roof of the car got bulged downwards."

"Direction has changed; we need to leave this place fast, Henry said and locked the car in fourth gear. The car jumped high in the air, over the road covered with heavy snow looking like the desert of the snow."

When Henry was driving, Olivia took the lever from the toolbox and bring out the spiky from his injured hand, came out with blood and little bit fresh flesh. The dark blood with the flesh was flowing from the hand and I yelled heavily in pain, that my voice became the echo in the ongoing world.

"Please all pick the hands of each other tightly; we are going to get collapsed with a heavy tree! Henry announced without any further initiative and tightens his seatbelt again."

"You can't do this, David yelled, wanted to stop him. This is my family. You can't do this."

"We would die" the car roof would bend down on us in few minutes. I am going to do this and you can't stop me, Henry replied.

And in just a few seconds the car got collapsed with the huge tree. It was really a huge jerk and we all got unconscious. A heavy sound teased our ears heavily and our heads were stuck with the random things inside the car.

CHAPTER SIX

Snag, Canada
    3:30 Sunday Afternoon
    Same day
Blood was everywhere on the seats. The whole car was looking painted with blood. Spiky Cone shaped ices were not falling from the sky at that time. There was a deep silence around us. No leaves were on the trees, in fact, flooded with snow and no sign people on the slippery road. Everything had vanished. My face was out the window, suddenly few cold drops fell on my face and I got conscious. I was trying to open my eyes but my eyes were not allowing me to do so. Everyone had fallen on their seats carelessly.

"Hey Olivia, Pearl, Ronan, get up! I announced with some hope. Everything has cleared. Suddenly the strange little girl and Henry got conscious."

"Are you okay? Henry asked me."

The giant iceberg on the roof of the car has fallen from the car. Now we were safe.

Before everyone got to wake up, I came out from the broken car and picked the collar of Henry insanely from my left hand. My right hand had paralysed already, controlling my pain but it was not more than the pain of my family.

"Get out from here with your girlfriend! We don't need anyone to save my family. What did you do? Are you really out of mind? You did this! I think you don't know the value of family! And I pushed him swiftly towards the car."

"I know the value of family, even much better than you, that's why I did this, Henry replied, much sad but not apologized. His tears were getting frozen in the cool snowy temperature. I have lost my mom in an accident; I lost my dad a few years ago. But you know they never told me to clever for the family, to behave cowardly for the family. It hurts much when you help everyone and no one comes out to help you. Isn't look strange? Don't go selfish for the family, be brave for your family, Henry continued while pointed his finger in my eyes.

"Listen, this is not the end, this is the beginning. Why don't you understand? This is Skyfall and he brings out the book and threw it in my face. Read this! The ice swords would fall in short intervals for two days and at last the whole sky would fall, the world biggest iceberg and whole Canada would vanish. All were stunned. We are in the womb of death. Only we can help each other. No one will come to help us."

Look around and see the buried frozen faces; they struggled to fight for themselves. There's no pit at every step, there's death at every step.

"Okay? Would we help each other? Henry questioned."

"Fine! I promised to expect a promise from him, but you don't take any decision without mutual consent except in case of emergency."

"Okay and we shook hands."

Hey you! Henry stopped. I forgot to ask your name.

Not strange, Mr I am Lenore, she replied in attitude. Look first we need to check what we have left? The weather is clear and this is a good opportunity to get prepared for our next step and everything, Lenore said and planned the strategy.

Okay! I and Henry nodded.

"And what about the owner of this bag? What would we have said?"

"So, you think the owner is still alive?"

"I don't know. Okay! Buy a water bottle for my daughter pearl. I know you can't. You can't do anything with this bullshit money. Keep this money, you can take it, but we can't take it, I announced, much frustrated inside."

An unending fight was still carrying on between us.

"But David, Olivia interrupted me in the middle."

"No Olivia, we can't take this money. You have lost happiness in me. I don't want to do the same mistake again."

"Okay, Henry gestured in lost attitude."

"The sun would not rise but morning will surely happen, Henry said virtuously. We need to leave this place as soon as possible. We have only the last day to save ourselves. We are going in few minutes.

"You know the way and where are we going? I asked Henry."

"Let everyone come inside the car. Henry opened the Skyfall book and found the page number 93. Look at this map, he said tonelessly and pointed his sharp finger towards the map. We would move towards north to find out the airport so that we can leave towards the USA and this is the only way to get rid of this Skyfall. Tomorrow the spiky cone-shaped ice would be much bigger and dangerous than before. Everything would get freeze as the temperature will go down to minus 80 degrees."

"Really? We sounded in unison."

But are you sure about this? I asked Henry.

I am not really sure about this! But I trust my Dad completely, Henry replied with some belief.

"Okay come inside we are going to move."

"Okay, we sounded in unison again."

CHAPTER SEVEN

Snag, Canada
8 o clock Monday Night
Same day

"The sun is not going to rise, Henry said. How would we feel when we come to know that we have to live only in dark? You love the rising sun?"

"It would be the biggest curse ever did to earth. I really don't know whether I love the rising sun or not. We love the rising sun still we appreciate the beautiful sunset, I replied psychologically."

"Is there any reason?"

"Really I don't have."

Everyone was sleeping carelessly on their seats. The tyres of the car were crawling on the slippery snow. Tyres were damaged due to the spiky cone of ice. There was too much black dark night everywhere. No stars in the sky, only dark night with the harsh sound of wind. It was like the snowy wind echoed itself and created the thunder in our mind. The headlights of the car were burning the fog so cleverly, making our way for little distance.

"Look at the sky, I yelled. Look at the sky! The dark black clouds are moving. Ice swords would fall from the sky anytime and before I completed my words, it got started."

It's much heavier and bigger than before. Everyone got to wake up with the scared faces.

"David, what happened? Olivia questioned."

"Ice swords are falling from the sky again, I replied."

"Hey! Stop the car, the Olivia groaned. Look ahead attentively."

There's nothing much clear, Henry frowned. He cleaned the layer of fog from the front glass and tried to see. Blood was sprinkled everywhere. The pieces of flesh were stitched on the hard ice carelessly.

"Hey, there's heavy crowd place? Henry announced mouth fell open."

"No no no! They are coming towards us, Change the way! Right now! I yelled. We stopped the car to take the reverse turn. We slammed on each other and the strangers were slammed on the bonnet of our car."

"Take back! Olivia ordered, covering children with both hands."

We were moving in the back gear insanely and didn't know where we were going.

They are no more human, they have become insane zombies now and they are trying to eat us. People have lost their mind due to extreme chill temperature. Their bodies were stitched with spiky cone-shaped ice swords. Their mind had frozen completely.

As our car was running endlessly in the back gear, it collided with the giant tree whose leaves were frozen, covered with ice and our car was like the giant iceberg. All the zombies jumped upon our car. Their voice was screaming us more than their hunting act. Everyone was gasping for breath, struggling to get out from this mess. Blood patches were stamped everywhere on the car and the front glass was carelessly rubbed with the dark red-black blood, reflecting red colour in the night.

"Move the car right now, I ordered and yelled."

"The gear has jammed, Henry replied, trying to unlock the gear."

"You have to move the car!"

"The gear has stopped working."

"All the zombies were upon the car, everywhere on the bonnet, screen and roof. They were trying to get enter into, scratching their sharp nails on the glass. I think their bodies have observed so many changes. They were not looking like normal human being.

We both applied our entire energy to move the gear. Our life was stuck with this gear.

"Move the gear, we howled."

Suddenly the gear got open. Henry swiftly puts down to third gear and three zombies got smashed in air high and some got crushed under the wheels of the car. The speed was good enough to jump like a child who got the balloon full of helium.

We jumped high in the air, paused in the air for few seconds and got vanished into the strange woods.

******

The car was moving automatically into the woods and we were taking the heavy breathing, struggling much with it.

"Thanks, man! You worked great! I congratulated Henry. Are you a doctor as well?"

"No, not at all, Henry replied, laughed a bit. Three years ago, we conducted an experiment on a 30-year-old guy with his permission. We put him into a box, to know how people would react when they go through extreme low temperature. We put his body at a temperature of less than minus Ten degree Celsius and the result was much surprised and astonished us. He had gone mad in two days. When we asked his name, he didn't remind his name.

Sometimes we have to conduct this type of experiment to save the world. I think sometimes it's good to save the whole world just by sacrificing the life of few people but we never want the sacrifice of the life of our family. Sometimes to prove the life, death should be shown, he exclaimed."

"You used a real human to conduct this experiment, I astonished."

"Nopes no, we did an experiment because he allowed us. He was suffering from cancer, Henry said."

"And what about his family? Olivia interrupted."

"He was an orphan, Henry replied, snipping the real-life thread continuously. He was at the last stage of cancer. We wanted to help him but God had the different perspective on that. He didn't want to live more. He got mad because he lost his family.

"We will die, Lenore, the media lady screamed and she grabbed her seat like a stubborn child, inside more terrified than us."

The car was moving like the jet, which lost its way. The bonnet of the car got vanished. Ice swords were hitting the front glass like a swift rocket. Suddenly the car gets close to the iceberg and the luxury car with screamed poor faces jumped forty feet high in the air. The sound was much dangerous than anything else in the world. It was like a rocket launcher and you are inside the world of fire. The journey was like the Harry Potter car, which jumped high into the air. The faces of everyone were totally blank, yelling and looking each other without any purpose. We were in the air, like wandering in the heaven of clouds. The moment we looked down, blow our mind completely. There was the giant deep gulf just above our car, flying in the air.

"We would die? Olivia screamed in the air."

"I don't know, Henry replied, eyes on the land. He picked the steering like he would leave it never."

After ten seconds of flying in the air, our car collided and crashed into the iceberg. We had left the woods behind but now we were on a peculiar island full of snow only. Just like the sea, we were not seeing anything around us. No Skyfall was happening there. The car had lost its lustre and in extremely bad condition. We were stuck inside.

"Olivia, Olivia! I screamed. My eyes were heavy after this dangerous ride. I saw towards the front seat, Henry was in partial dead condition. His head was flooded with blood, I saw it closely it was broken. I pushed him on the shoulder and he fell on the steering, waiting for the death."

"Hey, you can't die like this. I picked his hand tightly, dipped in his own blood."

Do you know? I said, hoped to save him. You dad was a brave man and you are like your dad, but you can't die like this. My eyes got heavy and hot tears were about to come out, even the strange girl picked his right hand. I could see the pain in little girl eyes. Everyone's eyes were in deep hope.

"Please wake up! She requested in the innocent voice. Please wake up."

His eyes were heavy as ours but still, he was breathing like an injured lion. His eyes were red swollen waiting for the death. He tried to speak out some words but his Voice didn't allow to and he handed over the Skyfall book into mine hand, dipped with blood.

"My dad was great. He wanted to save everyone but no one listened. I am giving you the legacy of my family. Now you can save the world. Tell everyone to save their lives. They are not aware of their death. I am extremely sorry but I hid a big secret. This Skyfall will not limit only to Canada but to the whole world. The whole world would freeze and only you can save the world, he said tonelessly struggling for breathe."

"But how, I asked."

But before he said something, he fell on the glass of the car. His eyes were shining reflecting my face, hoping for the help of the whole world.

"You can't die like this; I screamed and picked his collar. How can I save the world?"

He had given big responsibility on my shoulders. I was not in the good condition to save my family. All the gates of the car were flown away and we came out of the car. The car was in the dead condition but could be used only to take a good stay and get safe and couldn't be used to go further. But why would we stay? The chill wind could freeze our mind. We were seeing only the faces around us and couldn't able to see anything beyond two metres distance. Snow, icebergs everywhere. As we were confused so we came inside the car to look, what would we do next?

"We are stuck here David, Olivia said in disbelief."

"I know we were stuck here still we have to do something to save ourselves, I said. Temperature is going down each and every second."

"Ma'am calm down, Lenore said gave some hope to Olivia."

"We can't move in this heavy weather, Lenore insisted, searching for some positive feedback. We have to wait. We have to plan our journey otherwise we would freeze. We don't have food. We would die of hunger. We would die of thirst. We would die of shivering and our only hope is our planning, which can take us forward on this journey. We have to make a good plan; an extremely good plan and have to move forward in this tough situation, she demanded and took a deep breathe."

"So, do you think, we would get alive in this white desert, I questioned. I was much angry on her, maybe you can say me short tempered but this time she was saying something good, even extremely good but sometimes God plans much better than us."

"We have a strange girl with us even in injured condition. We don't know about her parents and even don't know whether they are alive or not, I gasped and said. Okay, tell me what your plan is?"

"I am really sad of the death of Henry but because of him we are here, she said in the low tone. Our plan is same so we have to move on. We have to bury his body in the snow. Hope he would reach the heaven in between this Skyfall. Jesus! Please accept him and help us, Lenore prayed, picked the book "Skyfall" in her hands."

"We have to move, otherwise we will bury under the snow, she declared again."

"But its minus ten degree Celsius now, Olivia interrupted in the middle. We don't have clothes which can bear this level of coldness. Our body will freeze at this temperature. Moreover, we don't have much power to move on."

"We have to move on, she replied. This car is now a waste. We can take out the soft leather and remaining stuff from the seats and rolled it around ourselves. This would protect us from cold winds and its great time to move on. Spiky cone-shaped swords are not falling and hope we would get something to eat in between the way.

Ronan was a little bit conscious pretended to be sleeping.

"Ronan wake up, we have to leave, I said. His hands had deep cut wounds which I want to cure too soon. We tore the leather from the seats. The leather and stuff were not much clean and partially reddish because of the blood of our wounds but we didn't have any other option."

We rolled the leather around each other and looking like cylindrical cans but it was not the time to both for it. We had to save us from the snowy wind. Tiny snowballs were still beating us on our faces but were not good enough to hurt us.

"We have to move forward and to pick the plane? I said, wanted to confirm everything. You are a media woman right!"

"Yes, she nodded, but what?"

"And they are waiting for us, I questioned again in attitude."

"We would go by private jet, she replied."

"You know how to fly? And even in this tragedy temperature"

"Really don't!'

"Then how would we go? Are you out of mind?"

"We should stay there, I think."

"You will die of shivering before hunger."

"Okay okay, but this is your last chance, I mumbled. Take everything that can help us from the car. "

"But there's only a toolbox, an empty water bottle and don't forget we have a bag full of money, I reminded few things"

Sometimes small things become big things. We have to move on now. We didn't have the watch but we know it was not the right time to stay here. Each and every second stayed here could bring the curse of nature.

"Bring this broken bonnet; put all stuff on it. Take the cloth and tied it around both ends and you have to pull this, she ordered me."

"Okay I can, I nodded my frozen head little bit."

CHAPTER NINE

Snag, Canada

2 o clock Monday Dark Night

We were walking slowly; appeared to be crawling on the soft snow going to hard early. My son Ronan was cuddled with my left hand and my daughter with my right hand and Olivia was walking endlessly with us without any expectation.

We have to move in the north direction; Lenore pointed his finger towards some direction while looking at the map. Unfortunately, we heard the crackling sound from the sky and my both loved ones grabbed me tightly. It was like they were giving me shield from both the sides but in fact, I wanted to.

Darkness was about to start in just a few minutes. Our legs were not much good now to bear our weight. Heartbeats were heavy reminding us that we are alive. The temperature was declining even our bodies were tired of our mind.

"We need to stay here, I requested."

"But how can we stay? We have to move continuously otherwise we would not reach the airport, Lenore replied."

"We need to stay here, Olivia interrupted in between us. Our children are not in the position to walk a single step anymore. Nothing is clear ahead. We are hardly seeing only five metres far away from us."

"Our minds were not in the good condition to think and we got inside to save us, just to save us and he closed the door swiftly."

There was a girl laid just opposite to us, in the unconscious condition. Her eyes were closed and an oxygen mask was attached to his nose. Her brown hairs were carelessly on the white bed sheet.

"What happened to her? Lenore asked curiously. I don't know why she always ready to poke her nose in every matter but somewhere she was fulfilling the responsibility of a human. Just before half an hour, she saved us from the tremendous weather."

"She is going to die, the strange man replied."

"And before we said something, someone pointed the gun at my wounded head. My breathes got heavy. Hey, what are you doing? I yelled, tried to save myself."

"I really don't know from where you are coming and who are you but you have to help me, the woman ordered, who targeted the gun on my head. She was the woman with end number of wrinkled on her face; skin got heavy and parallel lines on her head."

"You are asking for help? Just pointing a gun at my husband, Olivia interrupted to save myself. It's purely like the threat."

I was still happy as Olivia still saw me like her good husband.

"Okay you can say this threat, we don't bother but you are going to help me, she said, tightens her hands and makes the grip on the gun."

"You can't do this, Lenore said."

I can, the woman replied. The girl you are seeing is my daughter who has injured two days ago in this Skyfall and she disclosed her head. It was heavily stitched with the end number of black threads. The man you are seeing is my husband, Dr. Carl. We need blood for our daughter, otherwise, she would die. You don't have any other option. I will kill you and this time no one can stop us.

"Really! Okay, you can take, I agreed without any thinking. My heart was melted for the strange girl and I didn't know why."

"No no, David! Are you mad? Olivia yelled. You are already injured. You are not going to do this! Please!"

"We need three litres of the blood of O blood group, the lips of the strange woman mumbled, ignoring Olivia."

"Hey what you said? Lenore stunned. Three litres! I think you had not read the medical books clearly. He will die. We can't do this."

David's mouth got stitched because he was the only one of O blood group.

"We can't do this; Olivia declared." Her words broke down the strange woman and gun fell from her hands."

There's no bullet in this gun, and tears fell down from her wrinkled cheeks. We love our daughter very much. We adopted it still we love her more than our child. We need blood to save her, and she sobbed, tried to control her tears.

"I will do this, and I took the oath."

"You will die, Olivia yelled at me."

"Just before we were dying. This man helped us without taking care of his life. I am doing this and you can't stop me."

Dad, pearl took me to the emotional space.

"Dear! Nothing will happen, I gave some hope to her but inside I know after doing this I will be partially dead, I think almost dead."

"We are stuck here for Three days, asking help from everyone but I think no one left, the strange woman said.

By the way, where were you going?"

"We are going to the airport, Lenore answered."

"Airport? And she smiled cleverly. And you think the airport is all right. I think nothing has left but there may be some private jet if anyone of you knows how to fly in this bad weather, and then we can go."

"I will fly it, Olivia said."

"My mouth was stitched as I have lost the right over her, wanted to interrupt but it's much difficult to stop a brave woman."

"Okay, but we will go after the blood transfer; Dr Carl answered with a condition.

"Okay, I grinned and fell next to the injured girl. Do you have something to eat; I asked and smiled feeling weak inside."

"Yeah! We have bread but not the jam, the strange woman replied. We stole two bread packets from the departmental store. Of course, we can share some pieces with you."

"That's great! Please give some pieces to my family. They have not eaten anything for the last two days. I was speaking and in-between Dr Carl inserted the syringe into my skin to transfer the blood from my body to the injured body of the girl. Is it really strange that I never care for my family but my heart melted for a strange girl? Olivia's eyes were red swollen; I knew she still loved me. Girls never show love in front of a man but inside their fire is much bigger than us. Drop after drop my blood was passing from my body and I was losing myself in the unending dreams of my galaxies. My eyelids got heavy easily allowed to wrap my eyeballs easily but Olivia's face was still in front of my eyelids, little bit wondered how simply I am losing my life. In just half an hour I was partially dead, but my slow breathing was good enough to tell the evidence of my life.

"Will he recover, Olivia asked the Doctor."

"He will, but it will take two days to get him out of it. We need to give him something to eat, otherwise he would come in danger of death, the doctor said. We have nothing right now except few pieces of bread. We can give him one bread in a gap of two hours. I have some medicines which I would give him at the right time. It would help him to recover fast."

"Okay! Thank you, sir, Olivia replied tonelessly. When will we move to the airport?"

"Just in half an hour, till now we can relax inside the van, Dr. replied."

"Our heads were laid on each other carelessly and totally unconscious not even able to notice the voice of Skyfall. We were feeling the world cheapest thing, the sleep still feeling like the millionaire."

"This man is too honest and a good human being, the strange woman asked his husband. I have never seen such good guy in my life. Her wife is much lucky to have this kind of husband.

Olivia's eyes were closed but she was listening to the conversation carefully and I think we never trust the person till we see him sacrificing for him. We can't die just to prove that we can die for them but I have crossed everything in my life. I know Olivia loves me but she will never express because girls always want the boys to express their sacred love and sometimes it happens much dangerously.

"Right dear! The doctor replied while taking the intense breathes."

CHAPTER TEN

Snag, Canada

6 o clock Monday Early Morning

We were sleeping in the ambulance unaware of the dangerous fact. Our eyes were still scared even when we were sleeping. Nothing had happened well in the last few days. We have lost our baby, our home, our state and at last Henry, the person who helped us the most. Life was becoming much cruel to us. What did the God Want from us?

My blood was sucked from my body and fill in the body of the injured girl. My skin had become much delicate and skinny than before like a malnourished child but I had the only chance to save my family. I opened my eyes and everything looked blurry. There was nothing inside me except the last hope to reach the airport.

Olivia was not sleeping. When I opened my eyes, her face flashed even in my blurred eyes. We see the most loved person clearly even if we are blind. Nothing matters after that.

"Are you all right? Olivia said, putting her soft hand on mine. The feel was good enough to energise me. I wanted to hug her tightly for the last time but my body didn't allow doing so. I picked her hand tightly but suddenly we heard a voice. It was the voice of a private jet, flying high in the air without giving any indication. Our eyes were opened in astonishment. Everyone got to wake up as the sound was good enough even in this drastic weather. Olivia and others came out of the car and I was just waiving my hand from the window, feeling paralysed. As like in the movies it went without noticing us.

"We have to go to the airport right now, Dr Carl said, kicked the dust of snow aggressively. It must be going to the airport."

"Yeah! Olivia replied, agreed well. The doctor gets in the driver's seat but Lenore stopped her."

"Can I drive? She questioned."

"Obviously! You know? He asked her."

"I think you misunderstood me, she replied with the lavish attitude."

"Okay, he grinned and allowed her to drive."

"Tight your seat belts, Lenore announced."

"But there's no seat belt here, Olivia questioned."

"Then ready for the adventure, and she pushed the accelerator without showing any hesitation to stop it."

In just a few seconds it was talking to air and beating with the spiky cone of ices. We were waiving here and there and have lost control over us, like the van that has lost its brake.

Suddenly some spiky cone-shaped ices fell on the front glass of our vehicle and it got cracked.

"You must be a fire, oh God! Please drive slowly, the doctor screamed. You are not in the race. No one will award you for this."

"This is my slow speed. Hope you are not in the race with me. They awarded me a lustrous cup but this would award us life, she sounded freakish, turned the gear to fourth directly."

infected?"

"Infected? What are you saying? Lenore, astonished."

"Have you eaten the ice which is falling outside, he said picked the ice in his gloves. Look at this ice and the black dots freeze inside it, its poisonous ice. You all are infected; he said, making a big gap between us."

"You all stay away and wait for your death, the commando said cleverly. You listened, wait for your death."

Lenore was not ready to accept the decision; she threw the bag which we found in the car, full of million dollars.

"Take this money and rescue us, she ordered."

"Take this bag and get out from here, the commando said and threw the bag on her poor face. Lenore got angry and tried to harm him but we stopped her."

"Goodbye enemies, the commando waved his right hand and jumped to get his seat on the private jet."

"I know, we will not meet in future, still see you soon, the commando declared in attitude."

Yes, we will not meet, Lenore growled. Obviously, you will go to hell for this.

Lenore was yelling and Olivia fell on the floor with no further hope. Pearl and Devin were laid around her. She hugged her tightly reminding their end time.

We had lost everything. I was not in the position to support my body and fell on the slippery shiny surface and Skyfall book jumped from my pocket unintentionally and landed on the floor smoothly. Suddenly we heard the sound of the explosion. And when we looked outside it was the same plane that caught fire in the air even in the still wind.

"I think they reached the hell, the doctor said."

The pages of the book were turning continuously with the swift wind and I was starring it without any reason. The pages stopped flapping and reached the end of the page. It was the map of Canada hundreds of years ago which was created by the dad of Henry. I picked the book and when I zoom my eyes, gave energy to my body. It was miraculous. We were walking with our destiny but we didn't open it. Just near the airport, there was a hidden train which was buried hundred years ago but no one knew about that ancient train.

"Hey, I have good news, I yelled."

Everyone got alert.

"What happened? Lenore said with no interest."

"There's a train which was buried 100 years ago with the last Skyfall. If we find out we would get out from here, I replied in enthusiastic attitude."

"But we are infected now, the doctor said.

Are you a doctor, right? Lenore said sarcastically."

Everyone gets just inside the ambulance and she again accelerated the van at swift speed. In few seconds we reached and came out from the van.

"Is this the place? Lenore asked me."

"Hope so this would be, I guessed, bent my knees to make a big cross bulged inside with the screwdriver.

Please give me a hammer and this time I stuck hard and we get the voice like we get in case of metals, it was sonorous. Our eyes got sparkled with hope. It was the huge success after so many days of struggling. After struggling for two hours we managed to make a good slide to get inside the train after opening the jammed door.

Everything was frozen and an ancient smell which was locked hundred years ago stunned us. We got inside and closed the door but this was not the end. Troubles have become our friends. Skyfall started. We looked from the gate and a heavy sound teased our ears. A giant iceberg fell on the train. I think it was the biggest Skyfall we have ever seen and our train got bulged inwards inside more than the speed we think. We got feared. It was like we locked into the chamber of ice and this was the biggest mistake we did. I wanted to regret this mistake but I think we were too late. The train was bulging inwards into the womb of the earth. To whom I save, save myself or to save my family. Who is much worthy? My life or their life. The gate of the train was fully covered with the ice except for some upper part.

"Olivia, go! I screamed and ordered. I said go now."

"We will not move without you, Olivia declined my order."

I know she would not move without me but she had to. Sometimes we have to take tough decisions to save our loved ones. Love is in the air, fused with light, so how small issues can deteriorate it. They were not ready to leave, so I picked both the legs of Olivia with my latent energy to move up, to get outside from the small hole of the gate of the train. She picked the outside way without any intention. I really don't know from where I was getting energy but sometimes when most lovable things are in trouble, we become fire even when the whole world is vanishing. I picked the Ronan and pearl in my both hands and threw it towards the Olivia to grab them and also the strange girl swiftly. It was really strange that I didn't know the name of the strange girl.

"It's your turn now, Lenore said."

"You should go, I said. We have just a few seconds left. Don't argue when people are stuck between life and death.

Her right hand was already broken and I wanted to save her. She picked me from my legs from one hand to support to reach the hands of Olivia and she grabbed me easily. I didn't want to leave that powerful girl, who taught me to fight without swords."

"Please give me your hand, fast, I said abruptly."

She gave me her hand; I hold it for few seconds. Suddenly the train got down. Her hand got separated from the shoulder and she went down into the womb of the earth. Her hand got slipped from mine and only her hand bracelet was left in my right hand. My heart fell down. How God can so cruel with the good human or we think that we are the good human. I fell on the snow without any hope, took the ice and rubbed on my face aggressively. I was reacting like mad. We were tired of saving us. We were going to be mad. My mind was not working well and wanted a new beginning but this had not really happened. We all were tired of everything. Skyfall has stopped but the extremely low temperature was still killing us. Nature has shattered our mortal bodies but our souls and heart. We were alive but inside completely dead wanted death for us. For the first time, I was completely attached to a stranger. My eyes were flushed with tears, wanted to see her alive but I forgot, the bitter truth is the real significance of life, reflecting reality each and every second.

Epilogue

After Five Days
> *Greenland Hospital*
>
> *9 o clock Morning*

I need some water and coughed a little bit, I said to the media reporter who was taking my interview.

She handed over the glass of water. I take it with my trembling right hand attached with one of the glucose bottles. I was in the hospital.

"So how you and your family came out from the train? The media lady questioned curiously."

I don't want to make the things round about. After the fall of the train, we stuck there in the snow for five days so that someone could save us. Our bodies were alive but our minds were frozen. Even we tried to eat dry ice at the extremely low temperature. We ate human flesh and the things which were frozen in the drastic wind. I really don't know the things we eat unconsciously. We never thought that the god has reserved our food before we were born; I said and sipped some drops of water with my clumsy lips.

"Where is Olivia right now? And where are your children, the strange girl everyone? She questioned again."

"Olivia is no more! I said, keeping my eyes down starring at my hands continuously. She died of heart attack. After this incident, she was suffering from the phobia of snow. There was ice around us everywhere. Everyone got died and I yelled at her, inside much terrified. My voice gave her a big jerk. Everyone got died. You have taken your interview, now you can go away."

She got scared and stood up abruptly. She has seen the ocean of pain in my eyes. She was leaving without saying

Skyfall Song

Lost in the world
    Of hope and war,
    I created my roar
    To live with love and hate,
    Still, I never understand my fate.
    Every time I saw her into my eyes,
    I always find her flying with the bees.
    I wanted to live forever,
    But never wanted to be clever.
    Once I lost in the world of snow,
    Inside terrified,
    Much cried,
    To save my world again
    For the second time,
    But it was mistimed,
    I craved,
    I crawled,
    To fight with my own thoughts,
    To understand her well,
    Even in this Skyfall,
    But I failed,
    Inside unveiled,
    I knew,
    I didn't lose her,
    I lose myself,
    And at last, I left with the strangers,
    A girl, who taught me everything,
    To unstring,
    From the life I never understand,
    Unfortunately, I lost into the same world,

Much howled,
To understand the deep lessons.
Don't see the world from the road,
You would end your life,
Living in the huge crowd,
See the world from the sky,
Then you will understand,
How high you can fly.

About The Author

Deepak Gupta is pre-eminently known for writing plain sailing, meticulous, and pragmatic Self-Help books. He's the author of **more than forty books** including **10 Principles to Beat Failure** that won **Google Best Choice 2018** & became **Top Seller on Google Play Store in 2019**. He has been garnering much acclaim for his **30 Minutes Read & 10 Principles Series**. Till now, he has received **490k+ readership & a lot of appreciation** from all over the world. He believes in writing & living best exceptional content from his subconscious mind. He loves to observe, absorb, and write on various social issues, inspirational truthful words, short stories, and heart whelming poetry. Also, he has travelled to many places in India like Manali, Rajasthan, Goa, Kolkata, Madhya Pradesh, Jammu, Dalhousie, and Mussoorie to bring descent originality in his work. He *releases new short books every month* to get readers to connect with the truth of life.

Deepak Gupta received his post-graduation degree from **Delhi School of Economics**. Also, when he's not writing, he can be found wandering on his **exquisite terrace garden**. He lives with his family in **Delhi, India**.

Keep in touch with Deepak via the web:

Instagram @authordeepakgupta

Facebook: facebook.com/authordeepakgupta

Twitter @authordeepakgup

www.ingramcontent.com/pod-product-compliance
Lightning Source LLC
Chambersburg PA
CBHW020740160726
47993CB00006B/2542